This book belongs to

Emilie Jayne Kirk

Millie Jayne Kirk

For Jo, with all my love.
T. B.

To Sam.
R. B.

First published in 2004 by Gullane Children's Books
This paperback edition published in 2005 by

Gullane Children's Books
an imprint of Alligator Books Ltd
Winchester House, 259-269 Old Marylebone Road,
London NW1 5XJ

3 5 7 9 10 8 6 4 2

Text © Tony Bonning 2004
Illustrations © Rosalind Beardshaw 2004

The right of Tony Bonning and Rosalind Beardshaw to be identified as the author and illustrator of this work
has been asserted by them in accordance with the Copyright, Designs and Patents Act, 1988.
A CIP record for this title is available from the British Library.

ISBN 978-1-86233-585-1

Printed in China

Snog
the Frog

For Emilie

All the best

Tony Bonning • Rosalind Beardshaw

GULLANE™
CHILDREN'S BOOKS

Beside a grand and
majestic castle was a pond,

and at the bottom
of this cool, clear pond
lived Snog the Frog.

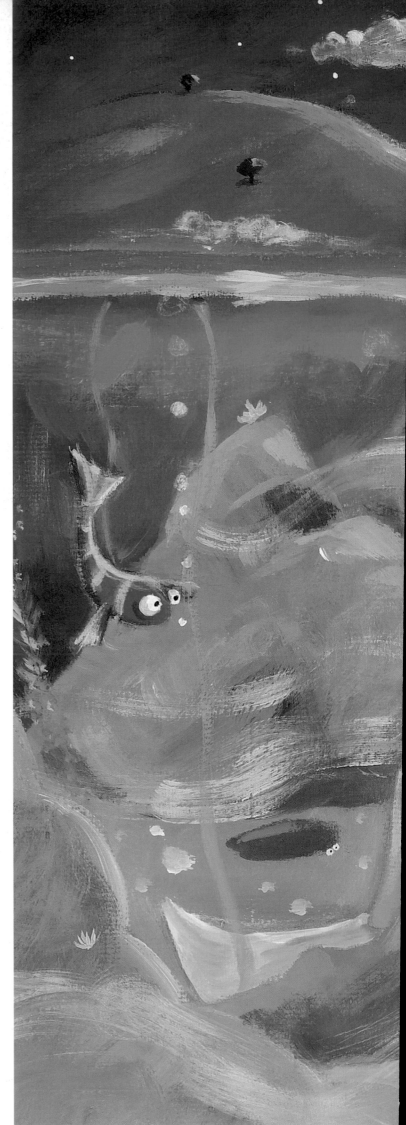

Snog the Frog climbed on his log and said, "Today is St Valentine's Day, and today I wish to feel like a prince. And to be a prince I need a kiss!"

With that in mind, he leapt onto the land and went

HOPPITY HOPPITY HOPPITY HOP,

until who should he meet, but Cow.

"Oh Cowy Cow Cow! I wish to feel like a prince. Pucker up your lovely lips and give me a kiss!"

"Who? You? Moo! No! Now go!"
"Oh! Just one?"
"No, go!"
And with that he went . . .

HOPPITY HOPPITY HOPPITY HOP,
until who should he meet, but Sheep.

"Oh Sheepy Sheep Sheep! I wish to feel like a
prince. Pucker those luscious lips and give me a kiss."
"Me? Meh! Baa! Nah! No!"
"Oh! Perhaps a peck?"
"Nooo, go!"

So with that, Snog the Frog went

    HOPPITY

    HOPPITY

    HOPPITY HOP,

until who should he meet,
but Snake.

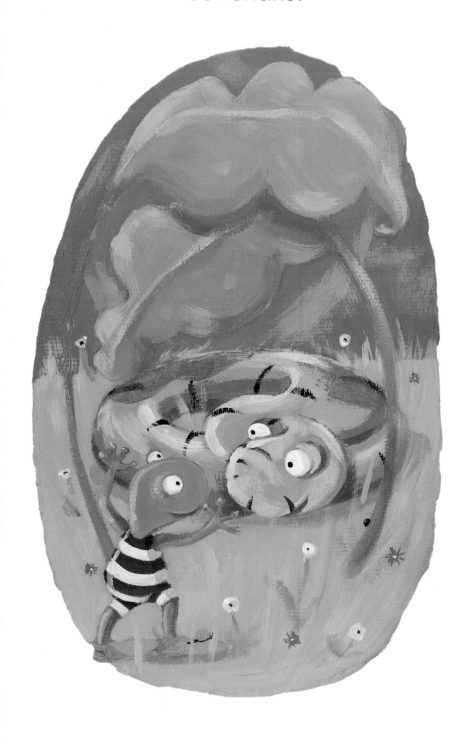

"Oh Snakey Snake Snake! I wish to feel like a prince.
Press those lean lips on mine and give me a kiss."
"A kiss, hissss, take this!"
"Oh no! I'll give that a miss."

And with this, he went HOPPITY HOPPITY HOPPITY HOP,
until who should he meet, but Pig.

"Oh Hoggy Hog Hog give this Froggy Frog Frog
a snoggy snog snog."
"What! Snort! I'd never kiss your sort."
"Spoilsport."

And with that, Snog the Frog went
HOPPITY
HOPPITY
HOPPITY HOP,

until who should he meet, but . . .

...Princess!

"Oh Princess, Your Highness, such happiness would I possess
were you to kiss me but once. Make me feel like a prince."
"Oh!" said the Princess, "I've read about this in the Fairy Tales.
One kiss and you turn into a prince."

And with this, she lifted Snog the Frog
and gave him a kiss.

"Alas, something is amiss.
The kiss has not turned you into a prince."
"Again, again, just one." The deed was done but . . .

nothing!

"Oh my!
Have one last try."
She did.

"I have tried once
and twice more since,
but you have not
become a prince."

"**No!**"
said Snog the Frog . . .

"But I feel like a prince...
and that's the main thing!"

Other Gullane Children's Books for you to enjoy

Big Yang and Little Yin
Angela McAllister • Eleanor Taylor

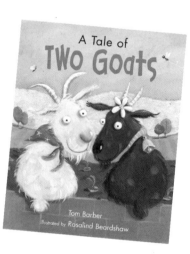

A Tale of Two Goats
Tom Barber • Rosalind Beardshaw

Don't Worry, Mouse!
Claire Freedman • Sally Hobson

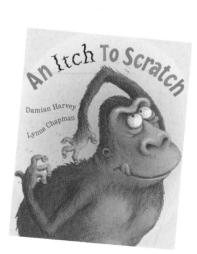

An Itch to Scratch
Damian Harvey • Lynne Chapman